Public Library
2

D0555990

Olive and Snowflake

written and illustrated by
Tammie Lyon

Marshall Cavendish Children

Marshall Cavendish Corporation
99 White Plains Road, Tarrytown, NY 10591
www.marshallcavendish.us/kids

The illustrations are rendered in soft body acrylics
and pencil on Strathmore Bristol Vellum paper.
Book design by Vera Soki
Editor: Margery Cuyler

Printed in the USA (W)
First edition
10 9 8 7 6 5 4 3 2

Marshall Cavendish Children

Library of Congress Cataloging-in-Publication Data

Lyon, Tammie.
Olive and Snowflake / written and illustrated by
Tammie Lyon. — 1st ed.
p. cm.
Summary: When her parents threaten to send away
the dog if he cannot learn to behave, Olive is worried
they will both be sent to live with a new family.
ISBN 978-0-7614-5955-2 (hardcover)
ISBN 978-0-7614-6069-5 (ebook)
[1. Dogs—Fiction. 2. Dogs—Training—Fiction.] I. Title.
PZ7.L99547Oli 2011 [E]—dc22 2011001124

For my parents, who always told me anything was possible; my husband, Lee, who has always been my biggest cheerleader; and all my friends, who make life fun. And especially for all the wonderful dogs I've known. Nothing makes life sweeter than the bond between a girl and her dog.

Olive and Snowflake
were the best of friends.

They played together,

slept together,

and read together.

In fact, they did everything together, including . . .

. . . getting into trouble!

When Olive left her banana peel on the floor, Snowflake hid it under the sofa.

"**OLIVE! SNOWFLAKE!**" yelled Mom.

princess
KITTY
RIN
TIN

When Olive didn't pick up her books, Snowflake shredded them into a million tiny pieces.

"OLIVE! SNOWFLAKE!" shouted Dad.

When Mr. Hardy was working in his garden, Olive and Snowflake raced through it.

"**OLIVE! SNOWFLAKE!**" Mr. Hardy groaned.

But the worst thing of all was when Snowflake knocked over Mom's favorite lamp.

"Look out!" hollered Olive, but it was too late. The lamp toppled to the ground with a loud **CRASH.**

"That's it!" said Mom. "I think it's time for obedience school!"

"Time to learn to behave!" said Dad.

"But what if Snowflake can't learn to behave?" asked Olive. "It wasn't all his fault. I was bad too."

"Then we might have to send him away to live with another family," said Mom.

UH-OH! thought Olive. *That means I could be sent away too!*

“What do you think I will have to do at obedience school?” Olive asked her best friend Emma.

"Well," Emma replied, "when my dog Moose went to obedience school, they made him sit, beg, roll over, and fetch."

"My parents said they would send Snowflake away if he doesn't learn. Will they send me away too?" Olive asked.

"Who knows?" said Emma. "You had better try hard to learn ALL the tricks!"

Olive sighed. "I hope I can."

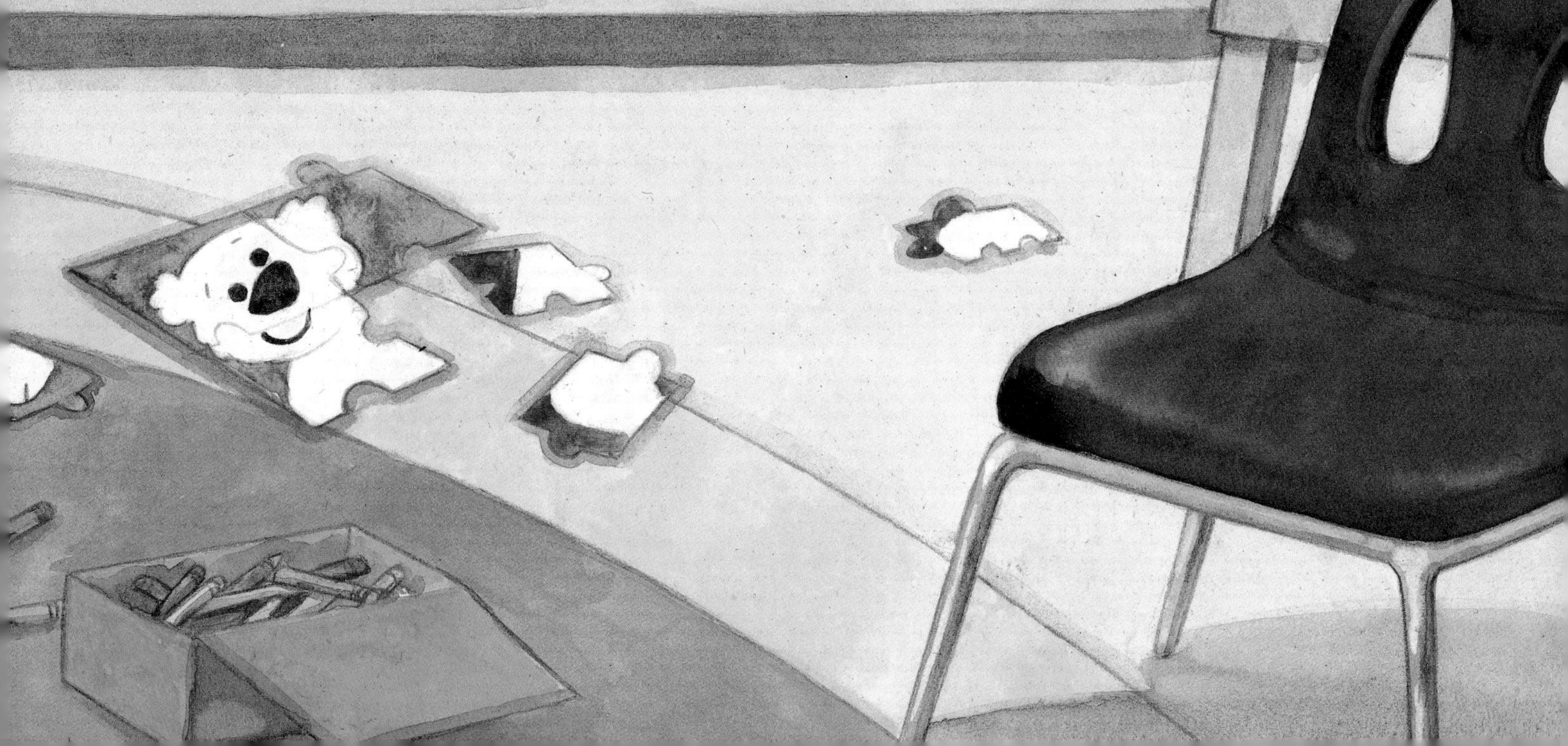

Today's
Sit
Stay

At obedience school, Olive, Mom, and Snowflake joined a huge circle of other dogs and their owners.

"I guess they've all been bad too," Olive whispered to Snowflake.

Just then, the instructor, Mrs. Greenlee, entered the room. After she introduced herself, she said, "First, we'll learn to sit and stay and then we'll work on rolling over and fetching."

Olive raised her hand. "I don't think I can learn these things. Maybe Snowflake can, but not **ME!**"

Olive's face began to wrinkle up. "**I DON'T WANT TO BE SENT AWAY!**" she wailed.

"Oh, Olive," said Mom. "Obedience school is for misbehaving dogs, not for misbehaving children. We would never send you away."

"Ohhhhhhh," said Olive. "I was so worried. I thought I might be sent away with Snowflake if I didn't learn. From now on, Snowflake and I will try to do our best!"

For weeks, Olive and Snowflake
worked very hard at obedience school.

They learned many new things and even a few fun tricks.

Most important of all, Snowflake learned to behave.

Now when Olive finished a snack, Snowflake helped her carry the trash to the kitchen.

When Olive finished reading her books, Snowflake helped her take them back to the bookshelf.

When they played outside, Olive and Snowflake helped Mr. Hardy weed his garden.

And best of all, Snowflake was allowed to stay!